Little Elephant

PHOTOGRAPHS BY
TANA HOBAN

STORY BY
MIELA FORD

GREENWILLOW BOOKS **NEW YORK**

The text type is Helvetica.
The full-color photographs were
reproduced from 35-mm slides.

Greenwillow Books, a division of
William Morrow & Company, Inc.,
1350 Avenue of the Americas,
New York, NY 10019.
Printed in Singapore by
Tien Wah Press
First Edition   10 9 8 7 6 5 4 3 2 1

Library of Congress
Cataloging-in-Publication Data
Ford, Miela.
Little elephant / by Miela Ford;
photographs by Tana Hoban.
    p.   cm.
Summary: Captioned photographs
depict a young elephant's adventures
playing in the water.
ISBN 0-688-13140-9 (trade).
ISBN 0-688-13141-7 (lib. bdg.)
[1. Elephants—Fiction.]
I. Hoban, Tana, ill.   II. Title.
PZ7.F75322Li   1994
[E]—dc20   93-25208
CIP   AC

For my mother, who waited for me   —M. F.

For my daughter, who was worth waiting for   —T. H.

I am a little elephant.

This is my mother.

She lets me play in the water.

First one toe,

then two.

A big splash.

Lots of bubbles.

Up goes my trunk.

Swing it around.

Under I go.

Can you see me?

Here I am.

Time to get out.

This is hard.

Oops!

Can I make it?

Yes, I can!

Hurry now.

Where is my mother?

Waiting for me!